A DAY WITH A BUS DRIVER

BUS
22

GRASSHOPPER

by Avery Toolen
illustrated by Dean Gray

Tools for Parents & Teachers

Grasshopper Books enhance imagination and introduce the earliest readers to fiction with fun storylines and illustrations. The easy-to-read text supports early reading experiences with repetitive sentence patterns and sight words.

Before Reading

- Discuss the cover illustration. What do they see?

- Look at the picture glossary together. Discuss the words.

Read the Book

- Read the book to the child, or have him or her read independently.

- "Walk" through the book and look at the illustrations. Who is the main character? What is happening in the story?

After Reading

- Prompt the child to think more. Ask: Would you like to be a bus driver? Why or why not?

Grasshopper Books are published by Jump!
5357 Penn Avenue South
Minneapolis, MN 55419
www.jumplibrary.com

Library of Congress Cataloging-in-Publication Data

Names: Toolen, Avery, author. | Gray, Dean, illustrator.
Title: A day with a bus driver / by Avery Toolen; illustrated by Dean Gray.
Description: Minneapolis, MN: Jump!, Inc., [2022]
Series: Meet the community helpers!
Includes index.
Audience: Ages 5-8.
Identifiers: LCCN 2021034095 (print)
LCCN 2021034096 (ebook)
ISBN 9781636903224 (hardcover)
ISBN 9781636903231 (paperback)
ISBN 9781636903248 (ebook)
Subjects: LCSH: Readers (Primary)
Bus drivers–Juvenile fiction.
LCGFT: Readers (Publications)
Classification: LCC PE1119.2 .T66328 2022 (print)
LCC PE1119.2 (ebook)
DDC 428.6/2–dc23
LC record available at https://lccn.loc.gov/2021034095
LC ebook record available at https://lccn.loc.gov/2021034096

Editor: Eliza Leahy
Direction and Layout: Anna Peterson
Illustrator: Dean Gray

Printed in the United States of America at Corporate Graphics in North Mankato, Minnesota.

Table of Contents

Driving the Bus 4

Quiz Time! 22

Parts of a School Bus 22

Picture Glossary 23

Index 24

To Learn More 24

Driving the Bus

Ms. Lisa's alarm goes off early.

Beep! Beep! Beep!

It is still dark out.

But soon she is out the door.

She has an important job!

She is a school bus driver!

Each driver has a bus
and a route.

The bus lot is full of buses.

Ms. Lisa picks up the key to her bus.

Her bus is Bus 22.

SCHOOL BUS

light

STOP

Then she checks her bus.

It needs to be safe to ride.

She makes sure everything works.

Good to go!

Ms. Lisa starts her route.

She drives carefully.

Ms. Lisa gets to the first stop.

She opens the bus door.

The stop sign goes out.

So does the arm.

Other drivers stop and wait.

SCHOOL BUS

STOP

arm

13

"Good morning, Ms. Lisa!" says Sally.

Ms. Lisa looks in her mirror.

"Hello, Sally! Buckle up!" says Ms. Lisa.

mirror

There are more kids
at the next stop.

"Good morning, everyone!"
Ms. Lisa says. "Find
your seats."

Once the kids sit down,
she will shut the bus door.

Ms. Lisa makes two more stops.

The bus is full.

The kids talk and laugh on the way to school.

18

"See you after school!" Ms. Lisa says.

The morning route is done.

In the afternoon, Ms. Lisa
picks up the kids from school.

She drops them off
at their homes.

"See you tomorrow,
Ms. Lisa!" Sally says.

Quiz Time!

What happens when Ms. Lisa opens the bus door?

A. the headlights flash   **B.** the stop sign goes out
C. the bus horn beeps   **D.** the windshield wipers turn on

Parts of a School Bus

What are the parts of a school bus? Take a look!

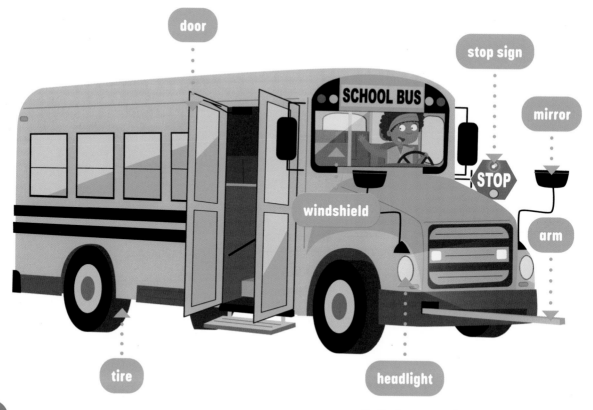

door

stop sign

mirror

SCHOOL BUS

STOP

windshield

arm

tire

headlight

Picture Glossary

alarm
A device with a bell or buzzer that wakes people.

bus lot
An area where buses are parked when they are not in use.

driver
Someone who drives a vehicle.

route
The path that someone or something regularly travels along.

Index

afternoon 20

arm 12

buckle 14

bus door 12, 16

bus lot 6

checks 9

drives 10

homes 20

key 8

kids 16, 18, 20

mirror 14

morning 14, 16, 19

route 6, 10, 19

safe 9

school 18, 19, 20

seats 16

stop 12, 16, 18

stop sign 12

To Learn More

Finding more information is as easy as 1, 2, 3.

❶ Go to www.factsurfer.com

❷ Enter "**adaywithabusdriver**" into the search box.

❸ Choose your book to see a list of websites.